nickelodeon

SPONGEBOB SQUAREPANTS
THE BIG HALLOWEEN SCARE

by Steven Banks
illustrated by Heather Martinez

Ready-to-Read

Simon Spotlight/Nickelodeon
New York   London   Toronto   Sydney   New Delhi

Based on the TV series *SpongeBob SquarePants*™ created by Stephen Hillenburg
as seen on Nickelodeon™

SIMON SPOTLIGHT
An imprint of Simon & Schuster Children's Publishing Division
1230 Avenue of the Americas, New York, New York 10020
© 2003, 2012 Viacom International Inc. All rights reserved. NICKELODEON, *SpongeBob SquarePants*, and all related titles, logos,
and characters are trademarks of Viacom International Inc. Created by Stephen Hillenburg.
All rights reserved, including the right of reproduction in whole or in part in any form.
SIMON SPOTLIGHT, READY-TO-READ, and colophon are registered trademarks of Simon & Schuster, Inc.
For information about special discounts for bulk purchases, please contact
Simon & Schuster Sales at 1-866-506-1949 or business@simonandschuster.com
Manufactured in the United States of America 0712 LAK
This Simon Spotlight edition 2012
2 4 6 8 10 9 7 5 3 1
ISBN 978-1-4424-4986-2 (pbk)
ISBN 978-1-4424-4985-5 (hc)

SpongeBob SquarePants was
getting ready for a Halloween party.
"This year I am going
to scare everybody," said SpongeBob.
"And nobody is going to scare me!"

"Hi, SpongeBob!" said Patrick.
SpongeBob jumped
when he saw his friend Patrick.
"Sorry, SpongeBob. I didn't
mean to scare you," said Patrick.

"I always get scared on Halloween,"
said SpongeBob. "Everybody calls me
SpongeBob ScaredyPants.
I wish I could be scary."
"Maybe you should be a ghost,"
suggested Patrick.

"Great idea, Patrick! I can be the
   Flying Dutchman!" said SpongeBob.
"Who is that?" asked Patrick.
"He is a very scary ghost. He comes
   every Halloween and takes
   people's candy," said SpongeBob.
"That sounds scary!" said Patrick.

"And I already have the costume!"
said SpongeBob.
SpongeBob took a sheet off his bed.
He cut out two holes for eyes
and put it over his head.

Then SpongeBob and Patrick went
outside in their costumes.
Some kids were walking by.
"I am the Flying Dutchman!"
shouted SpongeBob.

"I am the Flying Dutchman's
best friend!" yelled Patrick.
"Boo!" said SpongeBob.
"You look like the Haunted Mattress,"
said the little fish. "Ha! Ha! Ha!"

"I do not look like a ghost,"
said SpongeBob.
"You are right," said Patrick. "You
have a square head. Ghosts have
round heads."
"Wait," said SpongeBob.
"I have an idea!"

"Are you sure you want to do this?"
   asked Patrick.
"Shave me down. Make me round!"
   replied SpongeBob.
"And then we will go to the party!"
   said Patrick.

Everyone was having fun
at the Halloween party
at the Krusty Krab.
"I am a goldfish in a bowl!"
said Sandy.

"I am a witch!" said Pearl.

"I am a clown!" said Squidward.

"You sure are!" Mr. Krabs laughed.

"Where is SpongeBob?" asked Sandy.

"He is too afraid to come,"
replied Squidward.

HAPPY HALLOWEEN

SpongeBob and Patrick
were on the roof of the Krusty Krab.
"I am finally going to scare everyone.
This is going to be the best
Halloween ever!" said SpongeBob.

THE
KRUSTY
KRAB

Patrick lowered SpongeBob
down into the party with a rope.
"I am the Flying Dutchman!"
yelled SpongeBob.
"Give me your candy!"

18

Just then a jellyfish came by
and stung Patrick.
"Ouch!" said Patrick
as he let go of the rope.
"Help!" yelled SpongeBob.

"That's not the Flying Dutchman!"
said Squidward.
"It's SpongeBob!" said Sandy.
Everyone laughed at SpongeBob.

SpongeBob started crying.
"This is the worst Halloween ever,"
he said. "I am never going to
be able to scare anyone!"

"I am going home," said SpongeBob.
"Good-bye, SpongeBob ScaredyPants!"
yelled Squidward.

Suddenly the front doors burst open.
"It's the *real* Flying Dutchman!"
   screamed Squidward.
"I am the Flying Dutchman and
   I am mad!" said the Flying Dutchman
   in a booming voice.

The Flying Dutchman looked down
at SpongeBob.

"Who are you supposed to be?"
he asked.

"You," said SpongeBob.

"That is the worst costume
I have ever seen!"
said the Flying Dutchman.

"You do not think I am scary?"
asked SpongeBob.
"No! Spiders are scary!
Witches are scary! I am scary!"
replied the Flying Dutchman.
"You are not scary."

"What are you going to do to me?"
asked SpongeBob.
"I am going to eat you!"
said the Flying Dutchman.
"But first let's see
what is under that sheet."
He took off SpongeBob's sheet.
The Flying Dutchman screamed
and flew out the door as fast
as he could.

"Hey! I scared him! I am scary!"
   cried SpongeBob.
"I scared the Flying Dutchman!"
"I guess it was your pink hat,"
   said Patrick.
"That's not a pink hat.
   That's my brain," said SpongeBob.

"No need to worry! It grows back!"
yelled SpongeBob as everyone
screamed and ran away.
"Oh, well. Happy Halloween!"